AGENT ARTHUR'S DESERT CHALLENGE

Martin Oliver

Illustrated by
Paddy Mounter

Designed by
Paul Greenleaf

Series Editor: Gaby Waters
Assistant Editor: Michelle Bates

Contents

The Action Agency is a world-wide undercover organization dedicated to fighting crime and solving mysteries. Supremely successful, the Agency lives up to its motto, *Search, Solve and Survive*, by operating a "go anywhere, do anything" service.

Arthur is a veteran of three missions to protect the world from the Spider Organization.

Arthur's uncle, Jake Sharpe, is the founder of the Agency. As Chief Agent Controller, he has just sent Arthur and his trusty canine companion, Sleuth, on yet another action-packed mission.

You can join Arthur's adventure by solving the puzzles that appear on every double page. If you get stuck, you will find clues and all the answers at the back.

Arthur Arrives

ACTION CODE

All Agency communications
are in Action Code

⊖ θ ⊣ ⊢ ↑ ↑ < ≫ «
@ Symbols stand for different
   letters/digits each time
Symbol for A is shown in a
   yellow box. Letters B-Z, then
§ digits 0-9 follow in order, in
Π direction indicated by arrow
   on yellow box.
! / = space
¡ ! = full stop

Mission Instructions:
Travel to El Taco, find
main square and await
contact from fellow agent.
Local gang, the Scorpion
Mob, is working for the
Spider Organization.
Identity of their
leader is unknown –
see Crookfax of
villains at large.

CROOKFAX   Name :
STEVE GORE

CROOKFAX   Name :
BRIAN 'BABY-FACE' BOON
Well known bruiser and

CROOKFAX   Name :
BELLA DONNA
Notorious villain with
known Spider Organ-
ization links. Escaped
from Agent Arthur in
the Arctic. Current whereabouts
unknown. Beware : this woman
is dangerous.

EL FOR
LEATHER
ROPES R US

The travelling lasso-seller's cart creaked to a halt in a busy street in a dusty desert town.

"Welcome to El Taco, gateway to the desert," Agent Arthur murmured as he jumped off. "Stay alert Sleuth, we're on active service now."

Sleuth sniffed around suspiciously while Arthur tried to forget about his disastrous lassoing lessons and struggled to remember the contents of his mission dossier.

"We must head for the main square," Arthur said. "Any ideas where it is?"

Market Message

A few minutes later, Arthur followed Sleuth into the bustling main square. It was market day. Arthur took in all the strange sights and sounds and headed straight for the lively stalls.

"This is a good time to buy a desert disguise," he whispered to Sleuth. "You never know when we may need to blend seamlessly into the background. What do you think of this?"

Sleuth snorted in disgust but Arthur was proud of his new purchases. He was admiring his sombrero when he suddenly noticed a piece of paper clipped to the brim. The paper was covered in a series of unmistakable symbols – it was an Action Agency message.

What does the message say?

Trailblazing Through Town

After decoding the message, Arthur glanced around casually. The shady sombrero seller had disappeared. Now to dispose of the message.

As he waved it at Sleuth, Arthur felt warm breath over his shoulder and turned to see teeth chomping into the note.

"Yikes," yelled Arthur. He jumped out of the munching mule's way, slipped, and landed up-ended beneath a fruit stall. A street plan of El Taco fluttered gently out of his battered hat.

"Just what I was looking for," Arthur smiled groggily. "Now to meet our contact, Agent Andrea."

"This way," Arthur said, getting unsteadily to his feet. "Come on."

Sleuth reluctantly followed behind as Arthur strode down an alley and turned left.

"This map reading's so easy," Arthur thought confidently. He took the next right, skirted carefully past a cactus salesman and followed the alley as it led . . . back to the market.

"It's er . . . all part of my Action Plan to confuse onlookers," Arthur mumbled. "Which way now?"

Sleuth wagged his tail and set off. Giving a mule trader a wide berth, Arthur followed Sleuth out of the square and down narrow streets.

"Nothing must distract us from our mission,"Arthur whispered. "We mustn't waste any time."

Just then they walked past a food stall. Arthur stared hungrily at the snacks on display. Surely one mouthful wouldn't hurt. Ignoring Sleuth's warning growls, Arthur picked up a dish and took a huge mouthful. Everything went red!

Arthur blazed a trail over to a pump and gulped down gallons of water. At last the fire inside him was out. Now he could get back to his mission. But before he set off he thought back to the warning in the Action Agency message. Arthur sensed that something was wrong.

What has Arthur noticed?

Big Trouble

Arthur sprang into evasion mode. He raced down an alley until he reached a crossroads.

Which way should he go? Arthur had a great idea. Quick as a flash, he clambered up a drainpipe and onto a balcony.

But Sleuth was in trouble. Using his poncho, Arthur hauled him up. Just in time! Two shady figures appeared below them.

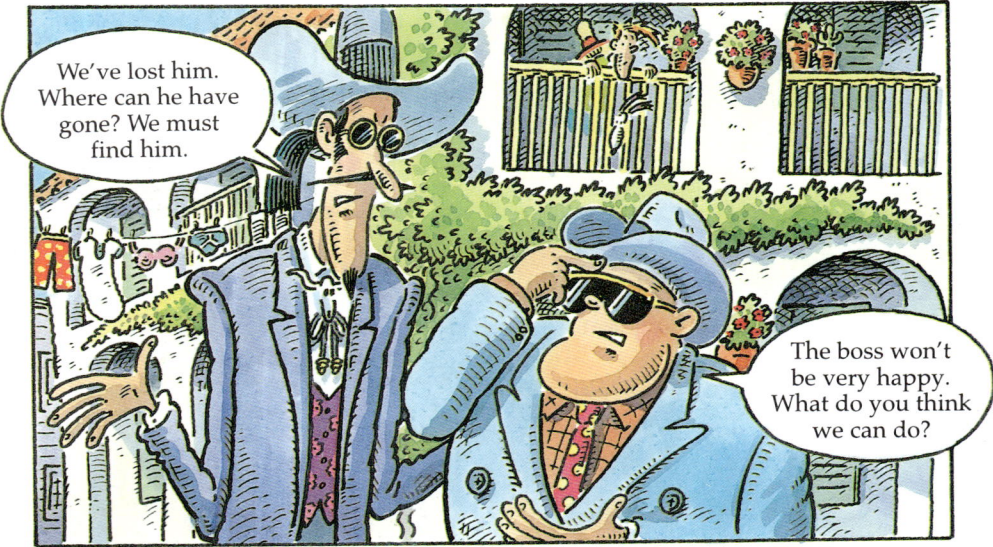

We've lost him. Where can he have gone? We must find him.

The boss won't be very happy. What do you think we can do?

Wishing his heart would stop beating so loudly, Arthur cautiously peered over the balcony. Directly below were the characters who had been on his trail.

Arthur remembered his mission instructions as he listened to the muttered conversation. The two men had to be Scorpion Mobsters, but who was their boss?

> One of you come with me, the other stay in case Arthur returns.

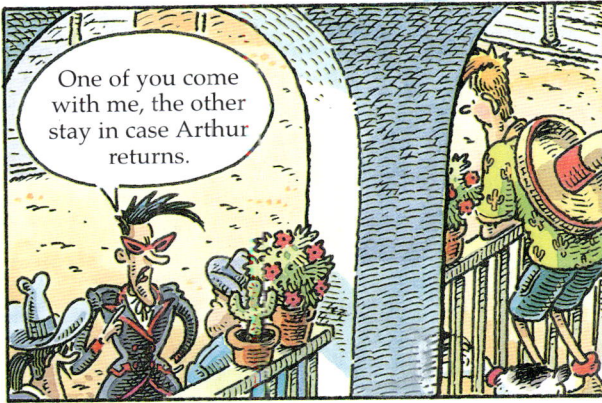

At that moment a tall figure marched menacingly up to the men. Sleuth's hackles rose and Arthur gulped as he recognized the woman. He had come up against her before. Arthur ducked down as he thought back to her Crookfax. Bella Donna was big trouble.

Arthur had to stay hidden until the villains had gone. But as he crept back out of sight, he knocked a flowerpot off the balcony . . .

.deonnaolp Soa fo
oeraoc neokat oeb
loliw oaerodnA
otneogA· moih foo
eSoopSoid dona
rouhtorA tonegoA
WoollooFSnooitoareopo
rouo poots otSuom
gnoihtoon,yodaeor
yloraeon eroa ew

SCORPION SIGNALS

TWO GREEN FLARES = IT IS SAFE TO PROCEED

ONE RED, ONE GREEN FLARE = ATTACK

TWO RED FLARES = DANGER, RETREAT IMMEDIATELY

ONE PINK, ONE RED FLARE = PROCEED WITH DIVERSION

Arthur waited for the angry shouts and gunshots, but nothing happened. He looked down and saw one of the Scorpion Mobsters out cold. Bella Donna and the other man had disappeared. Arthur and Sleuth jumped to the ground to check the damage.

Apart from a bump on his head, the villain was all right. Two pieces of paper had fallen out of his pockets. They could be vital. Sleuth checked that the coast was clear while Arthur began reading.

What does the message say?

Kidnap

Arthur was still trying to take in all the information he had decoded when he found that he had stumbled across the meeting place. There was a figure waiting by the statue of Il Desperado holding a red crash helmet – it had to be his contact, Agent Andrea.

Just then a car screeched to a halt. Arthur thought back to the Mobster's coded message. "Look out," he shouted, but it was too late. A bang echoed in Arthur's ears and a cloud of gas enveloped the statue.

Through the smoke, Arthur could just make out Agent Andrea being dragged into the car by two gas-masked men. The engine roared.

Arthur's brain raced. He pulled something out of his bag and sprinted over to the car. The woman behind the wheel was none other than Bella Donna! She snarled angrily and drove straight at Arthur.

SCORP 10N

At the last second Arthur dived out of the way. As he flew through the air, his right hand brushed the side of the car.

He hit the dirt, rolled over, and watched the car speed away in a cloud of dust. Sleuth was about to bound after the rapidly retreating villains when he felt Arthur grab his collar.

"Don't worry, they won't get away," Arthur muttered grimly, getting to his feet. "I had a little trick up my sleeve. I planted a radio beacon on their car."

Sleuth looked on in amazement as Arthur rooted through his bag and produced an electronic gadget.

"It's a top-secret tracking device, developed by Uncle Jake," Arthur explained, hitting the 'on' button. "The red line on the screen shows the route taken by Bella Donna and her crooked cronies. Now we must trace their path on the map."

By the time Arthur had found the map, the line on the screen had stopped moving. The kidnappers must have reached their destination.

Where are they?

The Plot Thickens

Uncle Jake's tracking device was a great success, unlike Arthur's map reading. He and Sleuth were hot, dusty and thirsty by the time they had arrived at Avenida Rodeo.

"They must have hidden the car," gasped Arthur. "It has to be in that building with the green doors. There's no time to lose. Stay alert, we're going in."

Just then they heard the screech of wheels outside. Arthur dashed over to the back window and saw two trucks racing off. He pulled at the door – it was stuck tight.

Arthur tugged and heaved the door open, but the villains were speeding away. As they swerved around the corner, a stream of objects fell off the last truck.

"We're too late!" Arthur gasped. "They've gone."

Sleuth found a way in through a broken plank in a side door. He growled the all-clear and Arthur crept inside to join him.

"Bingo! There's the car. Well done, Sleuth," Arthur muttered. "Keep an eye open for Bella Donna. Once we've rescued Agent Andrea, we'll try to find out what the Scorpion Mob is planning to do next."

AGENT ARTHUR'S ARCTIC ADVENTURE

Arthur had to follow, but where were they going? He looked around at all the empty boxes and open drawers and his heart sank. Bella Donna had done a good job at clearing up her operation.

Suddenly Sleuth barked, and pawed at something. It was a red crash helmet – the one Agent Andrea had been carrying. Arthur picked it up. It was much heavier than he expected, unless . . .

"It must be a special Action Agency helmet," he said, tearing open the inner lining. Photos, a diary and two coded messages came spilling out.

"This must be Agent Andrea's vital information. I have a hunch that it will tell us where Bella Donna is heading."

What do the papers say?
Where is Bella Donna heading?

Into the Desert

Arthur now knew where the Scorpions were heading and he was certain that they had taken Andrea with them. If he gave chase, he could rescue his fellow agent and maybe foil the Scorpion Mob's attack too.

But before Arthur could move, Sleuth dropped something at his feet. It was a stone-like object with a cactus shape in it that had fallen off the back of the villains' truck. What could it be? There was no time to ponder the question now. They had to locate the jeep that Andrea had mentioned in her log.

They found it easily. Arthur checked the survival equipment in the back, then he pulled out his Action Agency Any-Ignition Key and started the engine.

He stamped on the accelerator and the jeep lurched forward. Sleuth clung on desperately as they raced through the streets.

"Don't worry," Arthur said. "There's only one road out of El Taco. We'll soon catch them."

Arthur's confidence quickly dried up in the desert heat. A burning breeze blew sand toward the jeep, making it difficult to see. An hour out of town, the road turned into a dirt track. As Arthur swerved to avoid the potholes, he didn't notice the maps flying off the back of the jeep.

On and on they drove. Arthur followed the road ahead while Sleuth kept a look-out for signs of Bella Donna and her cronies.

They jolted along, and were nearing a crossroads, when suddenly the wheels on the jeep blew out.

They skidded to a halt and Arthur staggered out. The blow-out had buckled the axle and the jeep was beyond repair. On the road Arthur saw shards of glass.

"This is Bella Donna's work," he muttered. "But she won't stop us."

Arthur was about to search for the maps when he spotted Sleuth by the remains of a signpost. He dashed over to him and quickly realized the way that they should go to get to the refinery.

Which way is it?

Through the Trenches

rthur packed a basic survival kit in a backpack and they set off. Sweat poured off his brow as he followed Sleuth down the rough track. Two hours and ten bottles of water later, they were still trekking as the sun beat down on the dusty duo.

"We must be nearly there," Arthur groaned between swigs of water. "Stay on red alert."

Just then Sleuth sniffed the air and growled. He bounded off the road and crept up a stony ridge. Arthur followed close behind him.

Arthur shielded his eyes as he scanned the scene. Down below, the channels of a river had dried up, forming a series of trenches. On the other side, they could see the refinery, guarded by Scorpion sentries. Beyond a wire fence, Bella Donna was striding into a hut.

"We must get into the refinery," muttered Arthur. "We can easily reach the wrecked truck, but then we need to find a safe route through the trenches and past the fence."

Can you find a safe route into the refinery?

Inside the Refinery

Sleuth bounded happily along the pipe that led under the fence while Arthur crawled after him.

"Be careful," he warned Sleuth. "Once we're out of here, we're in Scorpion territory."

Arthur squinted in the bright sunlight as they leaped out of the pipe. Keeping out of sight of the guards, he and Sleuth hurdled over a steel tube, raced over the sand and hit the dirt behind some rusty oil drums.

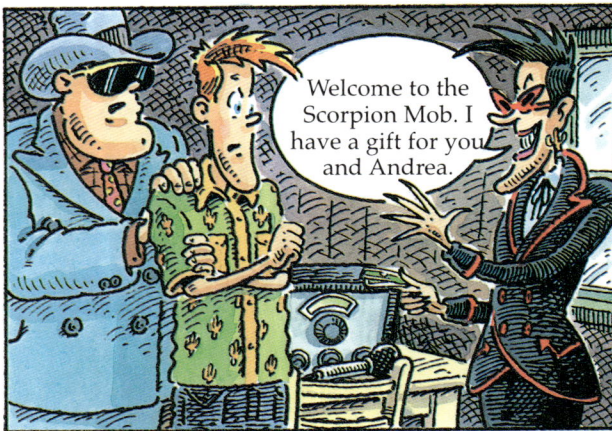

Welcome to the Scorpion Mob. I have a gift for you and Andrea.

aargh!

Bella Donna smiled evilly as Arthur was pushed into the hut. She hissed a strange welcome then thrust something under his nose. Arthur stared at two Scorpion ID cards – with his and Andrea's photos on them!

"You've fallen into my trap," Bella Donna gloated. "By the time you're found, my plan will have been a complete success."

Arthur heard a hiss of gas and everything went black.

The Action Agency is monitoring our radio frequency. They will have intercepted this message!

Grrrrr.

Arthur peered through the window of the hut he had seen Bella Donna entering. She was holding a piece of paper in one hand and talking in urgent tones. Arthur listened carefully to what she was saying to her henchman.

Arthur ignored Sleuth's warning growl. He was so busy trying to get a closer look that he didn't notice his faithful companion disappear with the backpack, or the dark shadow behind him, until it was too late . . .

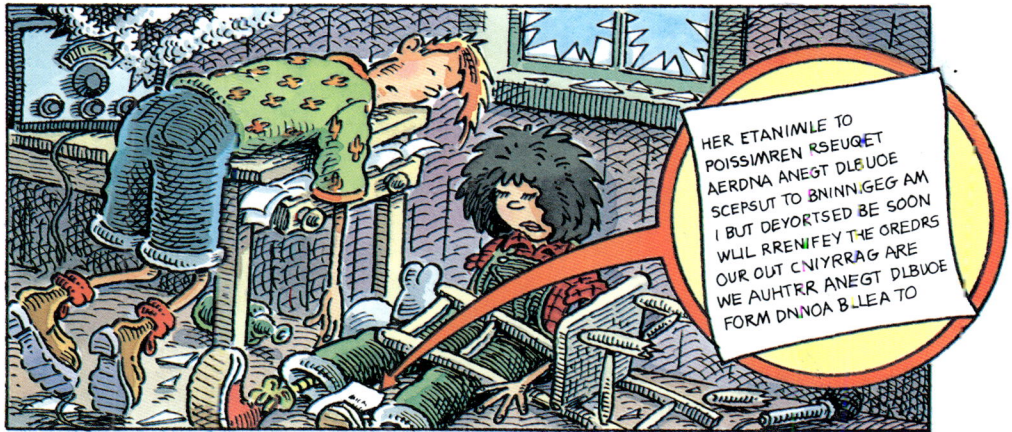

HER ETANIMLE TO
POISSIMREN RSEUQET
AERDNA ANEGT DLBUOE
SCEPSUT TO BNINN.GEG AM
I BUT DEYORTSED BE SOON
WLIL RRENIFEY THE OREDRS
OUR OUT CNIYRRAG ARE
WE AUHTRR ANEGT DLBUOE
FORM DNNOA BLLEA TO

At last Arthur came to. He rubbed his eyes and gasped. The hut had been wrecked. In one hand was his fake ID card, by the other was a cosh. Agent Andrea was slumped on the floor. Arthur knew things were terribly wrong.

Then he spotted Andrea's fake ID and the paper Bella Donna had been holding. If he could decode it, things might become clearer.

What does the paper say?
What is Bella Donna's plan?

Sabotage

Arthur's brain reeled as he pocketed the fake ID cards. Bella Donna had been trying to set them up. But what was all this about destroying the refinery? That must be what Operation Smokescreen was all about.

Arthur had to bring Andrea around first. He opened the hut door and dragged her outside, just as Sleuth appeared. Arthur bent down to pat him when BOOM, CRASH, BOOM, explosions ripped through the refinery. Arthur was blown off his feet and landed beside Agent Andrea. Her eyes opened wide in surprise.

"Agent Arthur?" she gasped. "What's going on?"

"S . . . sabotage. T . . . time bombs," stammered Arthur. "Look "

Andrea stared in horror at the refinery. The bombs had ruptured pipes and started fires. Oil was gushing out of the broken pipes, fuelling the flames. Already they were getting fiercer, and black smoke was billowing into the sky. The Agents had to act quickly.

"We've got to shut off the oil supply," Andrea said. "It's pumped along the pipes from the storage cylinders. But there's no time to turn off all the pipes, just the ones that are feeding the fires."

Which taps should they turn off?

Railway Repairs

At last Arthur and Andrea slumped down in the shade of a tall hut. It had been hot work, but they had beaten the flames.

Arthur took some swigs of water from a fire bucket, then told Andrea about Bella Donna's attempt to frame them.

Andrea turned pale when she heard the details of Bella Donna's devious plan, but then it was her turn to surprise Arthur.

"Operation Smokescreen isn't just about framing us," she began. "It's also meant to distract us from Operation Sandstorm."

I don't know the target of Operation Sandstorm. Bella Donna joked about a "training" mission, but that's all I heard.

A dust cloud could be seen on the horizon, heading their way.

"Help at last," said Arthur. But then an awful thought struck him. "What if the Agency has decoded the fake message and sent back-up Agents," he breathed. "We'll have a great deal of explaining to do."

"And by the time we've told them Bella Donna's real plans, Operation Sandstorm will have been carried out," Andrea said.

"You're right," Arthur agreed. "We'll have to thwart the operation on our own – that should prove that we're not double agents."

But first they had to escape through the desert. How could they do that when the jeep was out of action? Sleuth suddenly jumped up and dashed off.

"Follow him," Arthur yelled. "He may have an idea."

Sleuth led the agents past the charred pipes to a large shed.

"But how does this railway repair shop help us?" said Arthur.

"There's a railway line that runs from here to the coast," replied Andrea. "If we find the missing parts of this handcar, I can bolt them back into place and we can get away."

Can you find the missing parts?

The Journey Begins

A few frantic minutes later the handcar was ready and the Action Agents set off . . .

I've tightened all of the wheels

Keep quiet.

And I've found a map - we're ready to go.

We've done it.

Can anyone fix that squeak?

Squeak!

That's what I call a railroadrunner.

Wake up Arthur, it's only a dream!

Z Z Z Z Z Z

What a stroke of luck. We can hitch a ride with the train ahead.

But they were in for a shock. As they neared the train Arthur realized that they had run into trouble.

What has Arthur spotted?

The Sandstorm Express

Train Trouble

Arthur thought hard. Had the Scorpion Mob captured the train? Was this part of Operation Sandstorm? What was it all about?

There was only one way to find out. As the whistle blew and the train began to move, Arthur and Andrea sprinted across the sand and leaped for the guard's van.

Hang on!

Stay here, I'm going through this train to get some answers.

Z Z Z Z Z Z Z Z

Gasp!

Once they were safely aboard, Arthur came up with an Action Plan. Before Andrea could reply, he and Sleuth were gone.

They crept through the guard's van, past a sleeping henchman, and into the next carriage which was full of theatrical props, and dummies in strange costumes.

Arthur strode through the carriage but could go no further . . . the door was locked. He peered into the next wagon and gasped. It was guarded by two armed mobsters and was full of glittering gold bars! So that was what the Scorpion Mob was up to. They had captured the Sandstorm Express because it was a bullion train!

Grrr!

Just then Sleuth's hackles rose and in the distance Arthur heard someone moving around in the guard's van. The sleeping henchman must have woken up.

Arthur gulped – he was trapped. What could he do? There was no way out of the carriage without being spotted unless . . . Arthur suddenly had a brainstorm.

"What do you think?" he hissed a few seconds later. "As long as I've got the costume right, the guard will take me for a dummy, not an Action Agent."

Sleuth stared in amazement then growled. Arthur had overlooked some telltale details. He had to sort them out quickly.

What has Arthur forgotten?

A Risky Ride

You again - I'll finish you off myself.

Arthur held his breath and stood stock still as the villain walked past. It was all going well until the feather in Arthur's hat began to tickle his nose.

"I . . . I can explain," Arthur stuttered, but the Scorpion Mobster was in no mood to listen. He grabbed a sword, chased Arthur onto the roof and lunged.

Arthur opened his eyes in time to see Agent Andrea tying his dazed opponent to the roof.

"I don't know how you did that," gasped Arthur. "But thanks."

"That's OK," Andrea replied. "I could see that you were in trouble. Luckily none of the other guards have seen us, but why are all these Scorpion guards on this train anyway?"

Sweat poured off Arthur's brow as he parried just in time. Cold steel glinting in the bright sunlight, his opponent attacked again. Arthur fended him off.

They locked swords and Arthur was pushed back to the edge of the carriage. Soon he had nowhere left to go. The train sped on as he braced himself for the inevitable . . .

Andrea's eyes opened wide as Arthur quickly explained about the gold bullion aboard. That answered her questions, but what was their next step? How could they stop Bella Donna's operation?

"We must uncouple the train from the engine," Andrea said. "But that means getting to the engine cab without being seen."

Is there a safe route to the cab?

The Final Farewell?

After a hair-raising clamber over the train, Arthur, Andrea and Sleuth dropped into the engine cab. Nothing could go wrong now, or so they thought, but the train driver had other ideas. Arthur gulped as he stared down the barrel of Bella Donna's gun. Was it all over?

He didn't have to wait too long to find out. With Bella Donna's triumphant laugh still ringing in his ears, he felt himself flying through the air. He hit the sand then bounced and somersaulted down the embankment. On and on he rolled until he thudded into a very prickly cactus.

TOOT, TOOT. Arthur peered through watering eyes and saw Bella Donna waving from the train as it steamed off into the distance. Dustclouds marked Andrea and Sleuth's progress down the same sandy embankment.

Arthur limped over to the others. They were covered in sand but unhurt. Arthur winced as he extracted the last cactus spine from his body.

"So what do we do now?" Arthur said, as the sun blasted down on the tired trio. "Do we follow that train or just wait to be rescued?"

Hitched a ride on
the Sandstorm
Express at noon
and headed
directly out of
the sun.
We were on
train for about an
hour and a half.

In engine cab,
I noticed
speedometer
showing 40 MPH.

10 MILES

By my compass that middle rock is directly north of us.

"Neither," Andrea replied grimly. "Bella Donna will be miles away, and it could be days before we're found. We're running out of water . . . we must get more first."

Arthur knew Andrea was right – Bella Donna would have to wait. Right now the Action Agents had to work out their location, then head for the nearest oasis.

While Andrea was scribbling some journey notes, Arthur dug out his map and Agency Issue Compass. Then he began scanning the horizon for landmarks. There was no time to waste. Every second in the burning heat sapped their energy and brain power.

Where are the Action Agents?
Where is the nearest oasis?

Desert Challenge

Sunset

Night

Sunrise

Arthur blinked in the glaring sun. The nearest oasis was a day and a half's walk away. This desert trek really would be the ultimate survival challenge.

"Let's move," Andrea said, packing the backpack. "Water will be rationed until we reach the oasis. We must find some shade, then rest until it is cooler."

Arthur took a deep breath and they set off. The sun blazed down as the trio slowly made their way through the burning sands. Nothing moved in the shimmering heat, except for the Action Agents.

On and on they toiled. Arthur checked the map and compass while Andrea carried the backpack. Only Sleuth seemed not to mind the terrible heat as he gnawed on some interesting finds.

At last they collapsed under a parched tree. Andrea trickled out their water ration. Arthur swallowed gratefully and tried to keep his mind on the task ahead.

As the sun dropped, so did the temperature. The trio set off again. All night long they stumbled through the cold, desolate landscape . . . until once again the sun rose.

Would they ever reach water? Arthur wiped the thought from his mind and, ignoring his blistered feet, staggered after the others. They hauled their aching bodies onward until at last Arthur stopped to check his map.

Where was that oasis? Arthur squinted through red eyes and spotted vultures overhead, waiting for the kill. Nervously he licked his scorched lips.

"Maybe it's over the next dune," Arthur croaked hopefully.

They staggered to the top and, to Arthur's amazement, there was the oasis. They had made it! Arthur raced down the slope and was about to dive in, when he stopped dead. The oasis was dry.

What could they do now? Andrea poured out the last drops of water in a desperate attempt to refresh their drained brain power.

"We can't go on much longer," Arthur gulped. "We need water, and we need it now."

Andrea nodded grimly. As she scanned the horizon, something reminded her of Agent Zak's desert trek. Her heart leaped. Maybe they had a chance after all.

What has Andrea remembered?

Emergency Supplies

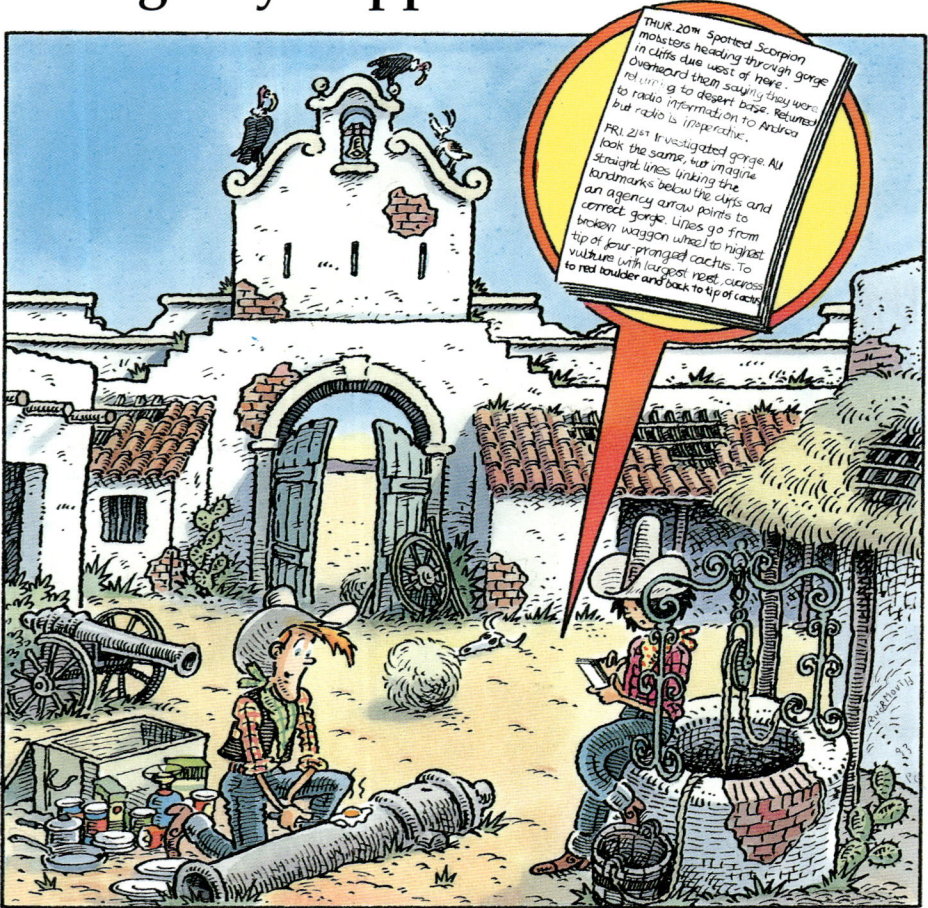

THUR. 20th Spotted Scorpion monsters heading through gorge in cliffs due west of here. Overheard them saying they were returning to desert base. Returned to radio information to Andrea but radio is imperative.

FRI. 21st Investigated gorge. All look the same, but imagine straight lines linking the landmarks below the cliffs and an agency arrow points to correct gorge. Lines go from broken waggon wheel to highest tip of four-pronged cactus. To vulture with largest nest, across to red boulder and back to tip of cactus.

Two sweltering hours later, the Action Agents staggered into the ramshackle fort. Sleuth sniffed around the courtyard, then he bounded through a door and into a small outbuilding. A few moments later he reappeared with an Action Agency Emergency Kit in his teeth.

Arthur rubbed his eyes. Was it a mirage? There was only one way to find out. He dived into action.

"This is delicious," Arthur sighed a few minutes later. "We couldn't have survived much longer without these supplies."

"You're right," Andrea nodded, between swigs of water. "But the supplies aren't all that Zak left. His mission log mentions Bella Donna's desert base. I bet that's where she is heading. If we reach it, we may find her, Agent Zak and the gold."

It was a good plan, but if they were to survive the next trek through the desert, they would have to recover from the last one. They rested in the shade and packed supplies. At last they were ready. Arthur took a deep breath, then they left the fort.

The sun shone down as the trio headed west. Picking their way through the spiky shrubs, they trudged through the rocky desert.

Eventually they came to a range of cliffs towering above them. At first it seemed they could go no further . . . but then Andrea remembered something.

"This is the place that Agent Zak mentioned in his log,"she said excitedly. "He got through one of the gorges. If we follow his clues we'll find out which one to take."

Which gorge should they take?

Desert Base

They set off in single file through the gorge. As dawn broke, Arthur spotted a gap ahead. They had reached the end. He was about to stride on when Sleuth growled softly.

"We'd better be careful," Andrea whispered, testing footholds in the rockface. "The exit will probably be guarded. We'll take a slight detour up this slope. Follow me and don't make a sound."

A few minutes later they reached the others at the top of the rock. Andrea was right, two villains were guarding the entrance to the gorge. Below them was a ramshackle town – it had to be Bella Donna's desert base.

"We must see if Zak is down there," said Arthur. "The gold may also be in the town. It's too heavy to move from the train . . . but where could they have hidden a train?" Andrea pointed excitedly to a railway track leading into a tunnel.

I haven't seen you before. Prove who you are or I'll take you to the boss.

A few minutes later Arthur smiled at Andrea. She had been right . . . they had found the Sandstorm Express inside an old mine at the end of the tunnel, but the bullion car was empty. Where was the gold?

The Action Agents began searching the mine, but they hadn't made much progress when . . .

They were interrupted by a menacing voice. Turning, they saw an armed guard. Had they come this far only to be captured again?

Arthur racked his brains. Then he realized that he had something that would get them out of trouble. He began to search his pockets.

What is Arthur looking for?

Agents in Action

I'm an old cowhand from the Rio Grande.

Yowl.

The gold is ready to be taken across the border. I need more men here in an hour . . . good.

No alcohol. Lemonade only by order of the Boss.

Arthur took back the fake ID cards from the guard, then followed Andrea out of the cave.

"Now to town," he said. "We must find Bella Donna and Zak."

Trying to act casually, the trio searched the town. They spotted Bella Donna in the bank, but first they had to find Zak and the gold.

They carried on with their search, peering into the saloon on the way. Just then Andrea had a flash of inspiration. It was so obvious . . . if Zak was a prisoner, he wouldn't be in the *bar*, he would be behind *bars*.

Andrea's hunch had been right, but how could they rescue him?

"I've got an Action Plan," Arthur muttered. "Just leave this to me." He flashed his fake ID and the jailer left them alone with the prisoner. Andrea unlocked Zak's cell.

"How . . . how did you? . . ." Zak began.

"It's too long a story," said Andrea. "This is Arthur and Sleuth. Do you know where the gold is?"

Zak looked puzzled. Arthur realized that they would have to search the town again.

They made for the door. Arthur stopped as he spotted a crowd of villains outside. The Action Agents braced themselves for a fight, but the Scorpion Mobsters headed past the jail and into a barn. Why?

"They've got more important things to do," Zak said. "They're going to drink homebrew. Bella Donna banned drinking but there's a secret supply in there."

"Those doors are the only way in or out," said Zak. "If we could lock or bolt them, the villains would be trapped, but how can we do it?"

How can they secure the doors?

The boss told us to take over guard duty.

Agent Andrea..!

Gunfight at the KO Corral

We meet again Arthur – for the last time. The rest of my gang are on their way but I will finish you off myself – draw!

While Andrea and Zak bolted the barn doors, Arthur began looking for Bella Donna. This time she wasn't going to escape. Arthur was determined to find her but it was Bella Donna who found Arthur!

The bank had been empty and Arthur was heading along the main street toward the KO Corral when his arch enemy appeared. Arthur squinted into the sun and gulped when he heard her familiar voice.

Bella Donna reached for her six-shooters. In a blur of motion, she drew the guns and fired from the hip. Arthur dived out of the way just in time.

He picked himself up and, keeping low, sprinted for cover. Bullets whizzed over his head and tin cans jangled as he collided with a wooden crate.

A hail of lead followed Arthur's progress. He dived behind a water trough and ducked as bullets, boxes and bottles flew around his ears.

Suddenly the firing stopped. Arthur peered out and saw that Bella Donna was reloading her pistols. On the horizon Arthur spotted more Scorpion Mobsters coming to pick up the gold. Arthur might just be able to take care of Bella Donna, but first he had to divert the newcomers.

What could he do? As Arthur racked his brains he glanced at the equipment falling out of a nearby box. His mind flashed back to something he had seen in El Taco. Maybe there was a way of frightening the villains off.

What is Arthur's plan?

Tying Up Loose Ends

Bella Donna laughed as the flares whooshed over her head and lit up the sky behind her.

"What sort of bluff is that?" she sneered. "There are no Action Agents to see your signal."

"It wasn't an Agency signal," Arthur replied. "Look behind you."

Bella Donna spun around to see her men turn tail and head off into the distance. Her jaw dropped in amazement, as did her guns. This was the chance Arthur had been waiting for.

Arthur knotted a rope and threw it, right on target. As the lasso tightened around Bella Donna, Sleuth collected her guns. Just then Andrea and Zak appeared.

"That's the loose ends tied up," grinned Andrea. "Now we can contact base and clear our names."

But Arthur frowned. They still hadn't found the gold. Where was it? Then he remembered the equipment in the mine and smiled.

Where is the gold?

Clues

You will need to hold this page in front of a mirror to read the clues.

Pages 4-5

Look at the Action Code on page 3.
A = △   B = ∞

Pages 6-7

Look carefully at all the people in the pictures up to now. Do any faces reappear?

Pages 8-9

First decode the message on the piece of paper, then get rid of any extra letters.

Pages 10-11

A piece of tracing paper could be useful here.

Pages 12-13

Try swapping over some of the words then thinking back to front.

Pages 14-15

Try and fit all the pieces of the signpost together. Remember that you know where Arthur has come from.

Pages 16-17

Look for a safe route under the fence.

Pages 18-19

Try working from back to front, then swap the first letter of each word with the last.

Pages 20-21

Trace the fires back to the taps.

Pages 22-23

Look carefully for five spare parts scattered around.

Pages 24-25

Are there any familiar faces here? Does the train's name ring a bell?

Pages 26-27

Look for any objects that a cavalier wouldn't, or couldn't, wear.

Pages 28-29

Keep a sharp eye out for guards. You must avoid them at all cost.

Pages 30-31

Use Andrea's notes and the map to lead you there.

Pages 32-33

Look back to the mission log on page 13.

Pages 34-35

Follow Agent Zak's instructions exactly.

Pages 36-37

Has Bella Donna given Arthur anything that might be useful here?

Pages 38-39

Can you see anything living around that they could use?

Pages 40-41

Look back to page 9. Can you see anything useful?

Page 42.

What was the equipment that they saw inside the mine? Have you seen any cacti growing somewhere that it shouldn't?

Answers

Pages 4-5

The message is written in Action Code. This is what it says when it is decoded:

MEET CONTACT AGENT ANDREA AT STATUE OF IL DESPERADO. SHE WILL BE CARRYING A CRASH HELMET AND HAS VITAL INFORMATION. MAKE SURE YOU ARE NOT FOLLOWED.

Pages 6-7

These two men have been following Arthur through the town.

Look carefully at the pictures on pages 4-7 and you will see them.

Pages 8-9

This message has been written from back to front with the letter "o" inserted after every three letters. This is what it says when it is decoded:

We are nearly ready, nothing must stop our operations. Follow Agent Arthur and dispose of him. Agent Andrea will be taken care of as planned.

Pages 10-11

Bella Donna and her cronies are heading for Avenida Rodeo.

Arthur knows that they started from the statue with the octagonal base.

By tracing the route from the tracking device and laying it over the street map, using the statue as a starting point, it is easy to work out where they have gone. The route is marked here in red.

Pages 12-13

In coded message one, the second word has been swapped with the fourth, the sixth swapped with the eighth and so on. The message is then written back to front. Once decoded, and with punctuation added, it says:

> From desert base to El Taco from Bella Donna. We must move soon. I will arrive in El Taco on Saturday to take charge. We will leave town and proceed with Operation Smokescreen on the same day, then we will carry out Operation Sandstorm.

Coded message two is similar but here the first word is swapped with the fourth word and the fifth with the eighth. This message is also written back to front. Once decoded, and with punctuation added, it says:

> From desert base to Bella Donna in El Taco. All ready for your arrival here. We shall expect you once both operations have been completed. Good luck with Operation Smokescreen. Your target, the Pumperoilo Refinery, will be taken by surprise.

From the second message Arthur realizes that Bella Donna is heading for the Pumperoilo Refinery.

Pages 14-15

Arthur should head in this direction to reach the Pumperoilo Refinery.

He can work this out by piecing the signpost together. When he stands the signpost upright, with the arm marked El Taco pointing toward the road he has just come from, he can easily work out where each of the other roads lead to.

Pages 16-17

The safe route into the refinery is marked here.

Pages 18-19

This message is written from back to front then, starting with the last word, the first and last letter of each word is swapped around. When decoded it says:

To Bella Donna from double agent Arthur. We are carrying out our orders. The refinery will soon be destroyed but I am beginning to suspect double agent Andrea. Request permission to eliminate her.

Arthur remembers Bella Donna saying that the above message had been intercepted by the Action Agency. He looks at the fake ID cards he was given and puts two and two together . . . he and Agent Andrea have been set up to look like double agents who are working with the Spider Organization.

Pages 20-21

In order to stop the fires, Arthur should turn off the taps circled here.

The other taps feed oil into pipes that are not damaged.

Pages 22-23

The six parts needed to complete the train are marked here with a cross.

Pages 24-25

Arthur recognizes the men as the ones who were following him earlier and knows that they belong to the Scorpion Mob.

He also notices that the train is called The Sandstorm Express. The fact that Bella Donna's men are aboard a train with this name makes Arthur certain that the train must have something to do with Operation Sandstorm.

Pages 26-27

Arthur has overlooked five things shown here.

He only has half a moustache.

How many cavaliers wore wrist watches?

Uncle Jake's tracking device is sticking out here.

He is wearing one normal boot.

His Action Agency Handbook is visible here.

Pages 28-29

The safe route to the engine cab is marked in black.

Pages 30-31

The Action Agents boarded the Sandstorm Express at a junction where two lines meet. Starting with this information they work out the rest of their journey from Agent Andrea's notes. Heading directly out of the sun at dawn means that they must have started their journey heading due west. Andrea noticed the train was going at 40 mph. They were on the train for an hour and a half which means that they went about sixty miles. By using the scale on the map, they measure sixty miles along the tracks heading in a westerly direction. Using Arthur's information that they are due north of a rock formation, they can pinpoint their position.

The Action Agents are here.

They joined the train here.

The nearest oasis is here.

Pages 32-33

Agent Andrea remembers Agent Zak's last report in her mission log on page 13. It was from a ruined Alamo fort below Horseshoe Rock where Zak said he had left supplies. Agent Andrea looks around and sees a fort below a horseshoe-shaped rock. She hopes that this is where Agent Zak left his supplies

Pages 34-35

The Action Agents follow Zak's instructions in his log and draw straight lines between the landmarks mentioned.

They form an arrow sign that points to the correct gorge. This is shown here.

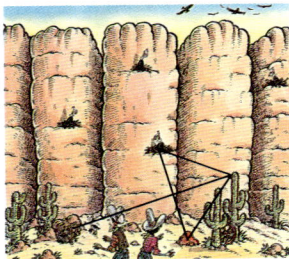

Pages 36-37

Arthur is looking for the fake Scorpion Mob ID cards that Bella Donna gave him on pages 18-19 and which he put in his pocket.

They should convince the guard that Arthur and Andrea are members of the Scorpion Mob.

Pages 38-39

In order to trap the Scorpion Mobsters, the Action Agents must secure the doors that are the only way in or out of the barn.
They can do this by closing the doors then using the log, the ladder and the saw as bolts by placing them in the brackets.

Pages 40-41

Arthur remembers the Scorpion Mob signals from page 9. Two red flares indicates that there is danger and to retreat immediately. Arthur sees the flare gun and box of flares and knows that if he fires this signal, the Scorpion Mob in the distance will retreat.

Page 42

Arthur remembers the cactus shaped object that he found on page 14 and the ones that he saw on page 37, along with paint pots and a furnace. Putting two and two together, he realizes that the gold bars must have been heated up, then poured as liquid gold into the cactus shapes. They could then be painted to look like small cactus statuettes.

Racking his brains, he remembers where he has seen these statuettes before . . . Bella Donna was surrounded by them in her room in the bank on page 38. So this is where the gold is hidden.

First published in 1994 by Usborne Publishing Ltd, Usborne House, 83-85 Saffron Hill, London EC1N 8RT, England. Copyright © 1993 Usborne Publishing Ltd.

The name Usborne and the device ♥ are Trade Marks of Usborne Publishing Ltd.

Printed in Italy   U E
First published in America August 1994.